KID POWER!

For Ruby, one very powerful kid!
Stay curious!

Written by Elizabeth Dozois
Illustrated by Stephen Dozois

MW00903023

About KID POWER!

This story is based on a program called **Can Do** that was designed and implemented by Ken Low in Calgary, Alberta in the 1970s and 80s. The **Can Do** program was designed to help kids:

- Explore human ingenuity

- Understand **how** and **why** to learn

- Build life-long learning attitudes and skills

- Cultivate a growing sense of confidence as a learner

- Develop a sense of personal power or self-efficacy

This book is dedicated to Ken Low and the work he has done to support adaptive learning in people of all ages. A portion of the profits from this book will be donated to the institute he founded, The Human Venture Institute (**www.humanventureinstitute.com**).

"Let's see if it's true!" **Oliver** shouted, bursting through the school doors. "There it is!" cried **Rema**.

She and **Oliver** raced over to a large boulder in the middle of the schoolyard. They'd heard that the kindergarten kids had moved it there – but how could a bunch of five-year-olds move something that big?

Rema inspected the ground around the boulder. "It must be true – you can see the drag marks!"

Oliver tried pushing the boulder, but it didn't budge.
"There's no way," he grunted. "Feel how heavy this is!"

"Let's ask my sister," **Rema** said.
"She's in kindergarten – she'll know what happened!"

Rema spotted her little sister **Akira** at the playground with her friend **Ellie**.

"**Akira**!" **Rema** hollered. "Who moved that big rock?"
"We did!" **Akira** said, jumping down from the climber. "Our class moved it!"

"And no one helped," **Ellie** said, beaming. "We did it ourselves!"
Oliver was skeptical. "Really? *How?*"

"A man named **Ken** showed us how. He says humans have superpowers – we just need to know how to use them."

Rema scowled at her sister. "Superpowers? Seriously? Who is this guy?"

"He came to our class during gym today," **Akira** said.

"And he let *me* turn the winch!" **Ellie** beamed with delight.

Oliver and **Rema** were confused. "The what?"

"The winch. It's this thing with a handle and a rope," she explained.
"When you turn the handle, it pulls in the rope. Kind of like a fishing rod."

WINCH

"Except *we* were the fish!" **Akira** said, laughing.
"**Ken** attached the winch to the climber in the gym. Then he told **Ellie**
to turn the handle while everyone else pulled on the rope."

"We pulled as hard as we could," **Akira** said, "but **Ellie** reeled us in – the whole class **plus** the teacher!"

Ellie smiled with pride. "That winch made me stronger than everyone else put together!"

"Mystery Solved!" **Rema** thought.

"So, you used the *winch* to move the rock?"

"Nope!" **Akira** said. "Be patient!"

"After the winch, **Ken** took us over to this huge block of cement and told us to try lifting it into the air."

"That thing weighed more than the *teacher*!" **Ellie** said. "There was no way we could lift it!"

"But **Ken** told us we could. We just needed to use our *superpower.*"

"What superpower?" **Oliver** asked.

"Creativity!" **Akira** said. "We can *invent* things that make us stronger and more powerful."

"Like winches!" **Ellie** added.

"**Ken** said that because of this superpower, the smallest kid in the class could lift that huge block of cement with *one hand*!"

Rema and **Oliver** looked at each other. Oliver shook his head. "No way," he said. "That's impossible."

LEVER

"A lever works the same way as a teeter-totter,"
Ellie explained. "It makes lifting easy!"

"**Ken** picked a boy in our class to lift the cement block,"
Akira said. "And guess what?!"

"He lifted it with one hand!"

"Cool!" **Oliver** said, impressed.

Rema smiled. She'd finally figured it out.
"So, you used the **lever** to move the rock?"

"Nope!" **Akira** shouted, giggling.

Her big sister sighed in frustration.
"Are you EVER going to tell us how you moved that rock?"

"We were just getting to that!" **Ellie** said.

"**Ken** took us outside to those big rocks over there," **Akira** said pointing to some boulders on the far side of the schoolyard. "Then he asked us to use our creativity to think of different ways of moving them."

"We came up with lots of ideas. Then **Ken** said, 'What about if all you had was a piece of rope - no machines, and no one else helping you?'"

"We were like: '**WHAT?** You want us to move that giant rock all by ourselves, and all we can use is rope?!'"

"Wow," said **Rema**. "He likes making things difficult!"

"Sure does! We said '**Ken**, we're only *five years old*. We can't move that thing all by ourselves. But he said '**You CAN.**'"

Oliver was stumped. "How?! How can you move something that heavy with just a rope?"

Akira smiled mysteriously. "By using a *different* kind of power."

Oliver was losing his patience. "What *kind?*" he demanded. "What kind of power did you use to move the rock?"

"**KID POWER!**" the girls screamed.

"Here's how it works," **Akira** said, giggling. "Let's say I want to move something heavy and I don't have a machine. Do you know how I can double my strength?"

The older kids stared at her blankly.

DOUBLE POWER!

"Get a friend to help!"

"**KID POWER** is all about cooperation," **Ellie** continued.
"If **Akira** can pull twenty pounds, then *together* we can pull forty!
And guess how many pounds a whole *class* can pull?"

20 KIDS=
20 x THE POWER!

3+2 =
3−2 =

"FOUR HUNDRED!"

"Seriously?!" **Oliver** asked. He was shocked. "400 pounds is *massive!*"

"I know, but it worked!"

"No machines. No older kids. No teachers. Just our class, using **KID POWER!**"

Akira beamed at **Oliver** and **Rema**. "*See.*
Even if you're five, you can do big things if you work together."

Rema was happy that the mystery was finally solved,
but **Oliver** was lost in thought.

Suddenly, **Oliver**'s eyes got really big.

"I have an AWESOME idea!" he shrieked. "**Rema**, go find us a giant rope.
Akira, you organize all the kids. **Ellie**, tell the principal to get ready."

"For what?"

"Kid power!" he shouted. "We're going to move the SCHOOL!"

BUILDING ON THE IDEAS IN THIS BOOK

Here are some ways to fuel your child's curiosity and help them experience the real-world power of mechanical advantage:

- Set up a hand winch and let your child reel you in.

- Go online to find videos of tow trucks or helicopter rescues to show your child winches in action.

- Put a shovel under a medium-sized rock and have your child push down on the handle so that the rock comes up from the ground. (This works best if you let them try to lift the rock on their own first.)

- Use a teeter-totter to explore what happens when you move a heavy load closer to the fulcrum.

- Look online to find plans for making a small catapult.

- Help your child to identify examples of levers in everyday life. (Hammers, shovels, wheelbarrows, and scissors are all levers that most of us use without ever really thinking about how they work).

- Think about ways to help your child explore other simple or complex machines in high-impact ways. For example, one of the most popular Can Do activities was the 'Kid Lifter' which involved attaching a series of pulleys to a chair and letting kids experience the thrill of lifting themselves into the air. (Use ratchet pulleys so that there's no risk if your child lets go of the rope, or explain the risks of letting go and spot them.)

- Get a bunch of your child's friends together and play tug of war with them. Have them try going one-on-one against you, and then let them see what can happen when they all pull at once.

- Model curiosity by exploring for yourself how everyday objects work and sharing your discoveries with your child. Excitement is contagious, so the more enthusiastic you are about your discoveries, the more your child will be.

About the Author

Elizabeth Dozois is a consultant working to address social issues in Calgary, Alberta, Canada. As an Associate of the Human Venture Institute, she also works with Ken Low and others at HVI to build capacity for adaptive learning among individuals, organizations, and communities. She is grateful to her brother, Stephen, for bringing her story to life visually, and to her family who love big, laugh often, fuel her explorations, and fill her world with joy.

About the Illustrator

Stephen Dozois is an artist and art instructor who also resides in Calgary. A fine art muralist for much of his career, he now focuses mainly on painting landscapes and urbanscapes of his beautiful province. His work hangs in both private and corporate collections. Stephen would like to thank his sister for the exciting challenge of illustrating her first children's book.

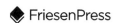 FriesenPress

One Printers Way
Altona, MB R0G 0B0
Canada

www.friesenpress.com

ISBN
978-1-03-916092-7 (Hardcover)
978-1-03-916091-0 (Paperback)
978-1-03-916093-4 (eBook)

1. JUVENILE FICTION, SCIENCE & TECHNOLOGY

Distributed to the trade by The Ingram Book Company

CPSIA information can be obtained
at www.ICGtesting.com
Printed in the USA
BVHW062247081222
653735BV00001B/1